SOCIAL PROGRESS AND SUSTAINABILITY

Shelter • Safety • Literacy • Health • Freedom • Environment

EUROPE

reword by **Michael Green,**
ecutive Director, Social Progress Imperative

By **Don Rauf**

SOCIAL PROGRESS AND SUSTAINABILITY

SOCIAL PROGRESS AND SUSTAINABILITY

Shelter • Safety • Literacy • Health • Freedom • Environment

EUROPE

Don Rauf

Foreword by
Michael Green,
Executive Director, Social Progress Imperative

MASON CREST

Mason Crest
450 Parkway Drive, Suite D
Broomall, PA 19008
www.masoncrest.com

Printed and bound in the United States of America

First printing
9 8 7 6 5 4 3 2 1

Series ISBN: 978-1-4222-3490-7
Hardcover ISBN: 978-1-4222-3496-9
ebook ISBN: 978-1-4222-8391-2

Library of Congress Cataloging-in-Publication Data

Names: Rauf, Don, author.
Title: Europe/by Don Rauf; foreword by Michael Green, executive director, Social Progress Imperative.
Description: Broomall, PA : Mason Crest, [2017] | Series: Social progress and sustainability | Includes index.
Identifiers: LCCN 2016007606| ISBN 9781422234969 (hardback) | ISBN 9781422234907 (series) | ISBN 9781422283912 (ebook)
Subjects: LCSH: Social indicators—Juvenile literature. | Europe—Social conditions—Juvenile literature. | Europe—Economic conditions—Juvenile literature.
Classification: LCC HN374 .R38 2017 | DDC 306.094—dc23
LC record available at http://lccn.loc.gov/2016007606

Developed and Produced by Print Matters Productions, Inc. (www.printmattersinc.com)

Project Editor: David Andrews
Design: Bill Madrid, Madrid Design
Copy Editor: Laura Daly

Note on Statistics:
All social progress statistics, except where noted, are used by courtesy of the Social Progress Imperative and reflect 2015 ratings.

CONTENTS

KEY ICONS TO LOOK FOR:

Text-Dependent Questions: These questions send readers back to the text for more careful attention to the evidence presented there.

Words to Understand: These words with their easy-to-understand definitions will increase readers' understanding of the text while building vocabulary skills.

Series Glossary of Key Terms: This back-of-the-book glossary contains terminology used throughout this series. Words found here increase readers' ability to read and comprehend higher-level books and articles in this field.

Research Projects: Readers are pointed toward areas of further inquiry connected to each chapter. Suggestions are provided for projects that encourage deeper research and analysis.

Sidebars: This boxed material within the main text allows readers to build knowledge, gain insights, explore possibilities, and broaden their perspectives by weaving together additional information to provide realistic and holistic perspectives.

SOCIAL PROGRESS AROUND THE GLOBE

Michael Green

How do you measure the success of a country? It's not as easy as you might think. Americans are used to thinking of their country as the best in the world, but what does "best" actually mean? For a long time, the United States performed better than any other country in terms of the sheer size of its economy, and bigger was considered better. Yet China caught up with the United States in 2014 and now has a larger overall economy.

What about average wealth? The United States does far better than China here but not as well as several countries in Europe and the Middle East.

Most of us would like to be richer, but is money really what we care about? Is wealth really how we want to measure the success of countries—or cities, neighborhoods, families, and individuals? Would you really want to be rich if it meant not having access to the World Wide Web, or suffering a painful disease, or not being safe when you walked near your home?

Using money to compare societies has a long history, including the invention in the 1930s of an economic measurement called gross domestic product (GDP). Basically, GDP for the United States "measures the output of goods and services produced by labor and property located within the U.S. during a given time period." The concept of GDP was actually created by the economist Simon Kuznets for use by the federal government. Using measures like GDP to guide national economic policies helped pull the United States out of the Great Depression and helped Europe and Japan recover after World War II. As they say in business school, if you can measure it, you can manage it.

Many positive activities contribute to GDP, such as

- Building schools and roads
- Growing crops and raising livestock
- Providing medical care

More and more experts, however, are seeing that we may need another way to measure the success of a nation.

Other kinds of activities increase a country's GDP, but are these signs that a country is moving in a positive direction?

- Building and maintaining larger prisons for more inmates
- Cleaning up after hurricanes or other natural disasters
- Buying alcohol and illegal drugs
- Maintaining ecologically unsustainable use of water, harvesting of trees, or catching of fish

GDP also does not address inequality. A few people could become extraordinarily wealthy, while the rest of a country is plunged into poverty and hunger, but this wouldn't be reflected in the GDP.

In the turbulent 1960s, Robert F. Kennedy, the attorney general of the United States and brother of President John F. Kennedy, famously said of GDP during a 1968 address to students at the University of Kansas: "It counts napalm and counts nuclear warheads and armored cars for the police to fight the riots in our cities ... [but] the gross national product does not allow for the health of our children.... [I]t measures everything in short, except that which makes life worthwhile."

For countries like the United States that already have large or strong economies, it is not clear that simply making the economy larger will improve human welfare. Developed countries struggle with issues like obesity, diabetes, crime, and environmental challenges. Increasingly, even poorer countries are struggling with these same issues.

Noting the difficulties that many countries experience as they grow wealthier (such as increased crime and obesity), people around the world have begun to wonder: What if we measure the things we really care about directly, rather than assuming that greater GDP will mean improvement in everything we care about? Is that even possible?

The good news is that it is. There is a new way to think about prosperity, one that does not depend on measuring economic activity using traditional tools like GDP.

Advocates of the "Beyond GDP" movement, people ranging from university professors to leaders of businesses, from politicians to religious leaders, are calling for more attention to directly measuring things we all care about, such as hunger, homelessness, disease, and unsafe water.

One of the new tools that have been developed is called the Social Progress Index (SPI), and it is the data from this index that is featured in this series of books, Social Progress and Sustainability.

The SPI has been created to measure and advance social progress outcomes at a fine level of detail in communities of different sizes and at different levels of wealth. This means that we can compare the performance of very different countries using one standard set of measurements, to get a sense of how well different countries perform compared to each other. The index measures how the different parts of society, including governments, businesses, not-for-profits, social entrepreneurs, universities, and colleges, work together to improve human welfare. Similarly, it does not strictly measure the actions taken in a particular place. Instead, it measures the outcomes in a place.

The SPI begins by defining what it means to be a good society, structured around three fundamental themes:

- Do people have the basic needs for survival: food, water, shelter, and safety?
- Do people have the building blocks of a better future: education, information, health, and sustainable ecosystems?

- Do people have a chance to fulfill their dreams and aspirations by having rights and freedom of choice, without discrimination, with access to the cutting edge of human knowledge?

The Social Progress Index is published each year, using the best available data for all the countries covered. You can explore the data on our website at http://socialprogressimperative.org. The data for this series of books is from our 2015 index, which covered 133 countries. Countries that do not appear in the 2015 index did not have the right data available to be included.

A few examples will help illustrate how overall Social Progress Index scores compare to measures of economic productivity (for example, GDP per capita), and also how countries can differ on specific lenses of social performance.

- The United States (6th for GDP per capita, 16th for SPI overall) ranks 6th for Shelter but 68th in Health and Wellness, because of factors such as obesity and death from heart disease.
- South Africa (62nd for GDP per capita, 63rd for SPI) ranks 44th in Access to Information and Communications but only 114th in Health and Wellness, because of factors such as relatively short life expectancy and obesity.
- India (93rd for GDP per capita, 101st for SPI) ranks 70th in Personal Rights but only 128th in Tolerance and Inclusion, because of factors such as low tolerance for different religions and low tolerance for homosexuals.
- China (66th for GDP per capita, 92nd for SPI) ranks 58th in Shelter but 84th in Water and Sanitation, because of factors such as access to piped water.
- Brazil (55th for GDP per capita, 42nd for SPI) ranks 61st in Nutrition and Basic Medical Care but only 122nd in Personal Safety, because of factors such as a high homicide rate.

The Social Progress Index focuses on outcomes. Politicians can boast that the government has spent millions on feeding the hungry; the SPI measures how well fed people really are. Businesses can boast investing money in their operations or how many hours their employees have volunteered in the community; the SPI measures actual literacy rates and access to the Internet. Legislators and administrators might focus on how much a country spends on health care; the SPI measures how long and how healthily people live. The index doesn't measure whether countries have passed laws against discrimination; it measures whether people experience discrimination. And so on.

- What if your family measured its success only by the amount of money it brought in but ignored the health and education of members of the family?
- What if a neighborhood focused only on the happiness of the majority while discriminating against one family because they were different?
- What if a country focused on building fast cars but was unable to provide clean water and air?

The Social Progress Index can also be adapted to measure human well-being in areas smaller than a whole country.

- A Social Progress Index for the Amazon region of Brazil, home to 24 million people and covering one of the world's most precious environmental assets, shows how 800 different municipalities compare. A map of that region shows where needs are greatest and is informing a development strategy for the region that balances the interests of people and the planet. Nonprofits, businesses, and governments in Brazil are now using this data to improve the lives of the people living in the Amazon region.
- The European Commission—the governmental body that manages the European Union—is using the Social Progress Index to compare the performance of multiple regions in each of 28 countries and to inform development strategies.
- We envision a future where the Social Progress Index will be used by communities of different sizes around the world to measure how well they are performing and to help guide governments, businesses, and nonprofits to make better choices about what they focus on improving, including learning lessons from other communities of similar size and wealth that may be performing better on some fronts. Even in the United States subnational social progress indexes are underway to help direct equitable growth for communities.

The Social Progress Index is intended to be used along with economic measurements such as GDP, which have been effective in guiding decisions that have lifted hundreds of millions of people out of abject poverty. But it is designed to let countries go even further, not just making economies larger but helping them devote resources to where they will improve social progress the most. The vision of my organization, the Social Progress Imperative, which created the Social Progress Index, is that in the future the Social Progress Index will be considered alongside GDP when people make decisions about how to invest money and time.

Imagine if we could measure what charities and volunteers really contribute to our societies. Imagine if businesses competed based on their whole contribution to society—not just economic, but social and environmental. Imagine if our politicians were held accountable for how much they made people's lives better, in real, tangible ways. Imagine if everyone, everywhere, woke up thinking about how their community performed on social progress and about what they could do to make it better.

Note on Text:

While Michael Green wrote the foreword and data is from the 2015 Social Progress Index, the rest of the text is not by Michael Green or the Social Progress Imperative.

SOCIAL PROGRESS IN EUROPE

*S*ocial progress is a society's ability to meet the basic human needs of its citizens, to create the building blocks that individuals and communities use to improve the quality of their lives, and to make it possible for them to reach their potential. This is not the same thing as economic prosperity, which is limited to money and profits and can give misleading impressions of a society's actual conditions. While development includes economic factors, social progress considers the many other things that affect quality of life, some of which can make life quite good even if a strict economic valuation would suggest otherwise.

The Social Progress Imperative measures various aspects of social progress in every country in the world for which data is available. The data comes from international organizations such as the World Bank, the World Health Organization, and the United Nations. The organization uses this information to create its Social Progress Index (SPI), which scores nations on how well they perform in three categories:

Basic Human Needs: *Does a country provide for its people's most essential needs?*

Foundations of Well-being: *Are the building blocks in place for individuals and communities to enhance and sustain well-being?*

Opportunity: *Is there opportunity for all individuals to reach their full potential?*

These scores allow the Social Progress Imperative to rank countries from the best to the worst and to arrange them in six groups ranging from Very High to Very Low social progress. Its rankings cover 133 total countries, with 1 the best and 133 the worst. Many other nations are unranked but appear in reports nonetheless.

History

Overall, Europe scores well on the Social Progress Index. Covering 3.9 million square miles, Europe extends from the Atlantic Ocean east to the Ural Mountains, the unofficial geographic dividing line between Europe and Asia. But geographic Europe is different from the countries that many people actually consider as European. Geographically, a large part of Russia west of the Urals is located in Europe, but Russia as a whole country is regarded as part of Asia and not Europe. The countries that are considered European are not just geographically close but bound together because of shared ideals and principles. The 48 or so countries that make up Europe operate under some form of democracy where people have a right to vote for their leaders. They also have free market economies. The exact number of countries that make up modern-day Europe may be debated because some countries that were originally considered part of the Soviet Union have now more closely aligned with Europe. Turkey's identity is a question mark as well. It is a country that straddles both Europe and Asia. It first applied for membership in the European Union (EU) in 1999, but it also has a strong connection to Asia.

Europe and Asia meet at the Ural Mountains.

About 300,000 years ago, prehistoric people known as the Neanderthals lived in the area now called Europe. As humans evolved over hundreds of thousands of years, civilization developed. They created organized farms, art, and forms of government. Minoan Crete may be considered Europe's first civilization. Beginning in 2000 BC, Minoan Crete had a sophisticated culture and trading industry. Over the centuries more nomadic tribespeople settled and developed communities. In the 8th century BC, Greek civilization flourished, with the first Olympic Games held in 776 BC. The ancient Greeks invented an alphabet and different types of mathematics. The people prided themselves on producing sophisticated sculpture, architecture, pottery, and other art. At this time, Homer wrote the *Iliad* and the *Odyssey*. Greek colonies spread to southern Italy and Sicily. In 507 BC a system of political reforms called *demokratia*, or "rule by the people," was introduced. In time, tribes settled into communities in what are now Italy, Germany, France, Spain, Denmark, and Sweden. But in the 8th century, the main area of cultural development in Europe was around the Mediterranean.

By the 3rd century BC, Rome had become the major economic and cultural force in the region. Like Greece, its government had democratic elements. But forms of democracy were to give way to monarchies in the centuries to come.

Western civilization begin in Greece.

By 30 BC, Rome took over Egypt and controlled the entire Mediterranean area for four centuries to follow. In the 3rd century AD, German tribes amassed along the borders of the Roman Empire. In the 4th and 5th centuries, many people began to migrate and populate more regions of Europe. The period was known as the *Völkerwanderung*, or "migration of the peoples." During these centuries civilizations developed that were built around the Christian religion. The great city of Constantinople, known today as Istanbul, was founded in AD 330. In time Rome shifted to become a hub of Christianity as well. After the 5th century, Germanic peoples in the north prospered and came together to form stronger groups. In the 700s, Charlemagne, or Charles the Great, united most of Western Europe, and the foundations of modern France and Germany took shape. Around the same time, an Arab influence from the south spread north into Spain and beyond. In the 9th through 12th centuries, the Vikings of the north invaded France. Normandy, in fact, got its name from the Scandinavian for "Northman." There were also Viking invasions in England.

Over the centuries, countries in Europe developed around a series of monarchies. Still, Christianity was the pervasive religion throughout the region, and it offered some teachings that promoted tolerance of one's fellow human beings. Perhaps from this foundation of belief a system of courts eventually developed intended to defend the rights of man. In 1215 the Magna Carta (or "Great Charter") was introduced in England. It contained 63 clauses promising all freemen access to the courts and a fair trial. It eliminated unfair fines and punishments and limited the power of the king. The Magna Carta established that the king needed consent of the royal council to levy or collect any taxes. This royal council gradually developed into a parliament and established the basis of modern democracy.

Over centuries all the European monarchies have slowly eroded, giving way to democratic rule. But the last genuine European monarchy, Luxembourg, did not end until 2009. Although Luxembourg had an advisory parliament, the country had been governed by a grand duke up until then.

Europe Today

Europe's population is fairly stagnant. It is increasing, but only very slightly.

Italy's health minister said the country was dying—its birthrate in 2015 is at its lowest since Italy's formation as a modern state in 1861. A total of 8.4 babies are born per 1,000 people. Some say the lower birth rates in Europe are related to economic turmoil and high unemployment in some regions. While fewer people are being born in some European countries, more immigrants are eager to come into European countries—especially with civil strife in Syria and Iraq. Instead of accepting population contraction, countries with declining citizenry could accept more immigrants, who could potentially generate more revenue and provide cultural influences. According to an article in YaleGlobal Online, Italy's population would decline by 15 percent by midcentury without immigration—even with immigration, Italy's population is expected to be 3 percent smaller in 2050 compared to today. Integrating immigrants into a country, however, can be challenging.

When it comes to social progress, many countries in Europe rank high on the index of the Social Progress Imperative, the SPI. Of the top 15 countries in the SPI, 11 are in Europe—Norway, Sweden, Switzerland, Iceland, Finland, Denmark, the Netherlands, the UK, Ireland, Austria, and Germany. Some European countries, though, don't do as well. France, for example, does well when it comes to meeting basic human needs, but the country faces challenges with environmental issues and with tolerance and inclusion of immigrants. Italy gets solid marks for taking care of basic human needs, but it is similar to France with weaker policies on personal rights, personal freedom and choice, and tolerance and inclusion.

Bulgaria is one of the poorest countries in the European Union. Formerly allied with the Soviet Union, Bulgaria joined the European Union in 2007, along with Romania. But Bulgaria's transformation from Communist rule to a free market economy has been slow. Organized crime and corruption have inhibited investors and growth. Still, Bulgaria shows great potential. It is a major grower of roses, which are used to make rose oils to produce perfume.

People dressed in traditional costumes sing and dance for health and a successful harvest at the Bulgarian Festival of the Roses.

Since the fall of 1993, many countries in Europe have joined together in the European Union. The EU grew out of a partnership of six countries called the European Economic Community (EEC). Formed in 1958, the EEC included Belgium, Germany, France, Italy, Luxembourg, and the Netherlands. The goal of the EEC was to promote economic stability and growth. In a similar way, the objective of the EU is to maintain peace and prosperity and raise living standards throughout Europe. The member countries also agree on policies that can help the environment, promote human rights, and allow for easy mobility to live and work among member nations.

One issue that the European Union is trying to help with is immigration. In recent years, Greece and Italy have taken in tens of thousands of immigrants from Syria and North Africa. The EU is providing relief to these countries to help take care of this great flood of people who are entering these nations. The EU has been developing plans to redistribute the influx of newcomers so Greece and Italy don't bear such a heavy burden when it comes to immigration. Germany and Sweden have also been leading the way when it comes to taking in these latest refugees.

Some countries are still considered as "emerging" after having lived through strict regimes. The area now known as the Czech Republic, for instance, was occupied by Germany in World War II and then controlled by a Communist regime until 1989. In terms of social progress, Slovenia, the Czech Republic, Estonia, Slovakia, and Poland perform very well in areas of nutrition and basic medical care, but they lag in health and wellness compared to other European countries. In many ways, these countries are catching up with nations that have longer, more established governments.

Ukraine is another country that was part of the Soviet Union but is now more closely aligned with Europe. In recent years, Russia has been in conflict with Ukraine. Because of the conflict, Europe and the United States have penalized Russia with economic restrictions. Russia is a major supplier of fuel to Europe, however, so these tensions have led to some instability in the continent.

Economically, Europe has been slowing. Unemployment rates in the EU have been above 9 percent in recent years, reaching 11 percent in 2013. Greece's economy has been especially hard hit in recent years, with about one in four working adults there experiencing unemployment. Greece has run up huge deficits—meaning the country has been borrowing a large amount of money and been unable to pay back its loans. Greece's troubles have rippled through Europe, affecting the economies in many other nations. Winston Churchill once said, "Never let a crisis go to waste." When circumstances force drastic change, it can be an opportunity. Some say that Greece now has a chance to get rid of failed economic approaches and promote entrepreneurship and innovation. In July 2015, Greeks voted against harsh austerity measures, but Prime Minister Alexis Tsipras felt forced to accept harsh spending cuts. After Tsipras's left wing party won a general election in September 2015, he felt he was given a clear mandate to lead.

Despite these current troubles, Europe remains one of the most prosperous areas on the planet, and many people who live here enjoy a high quality of life.

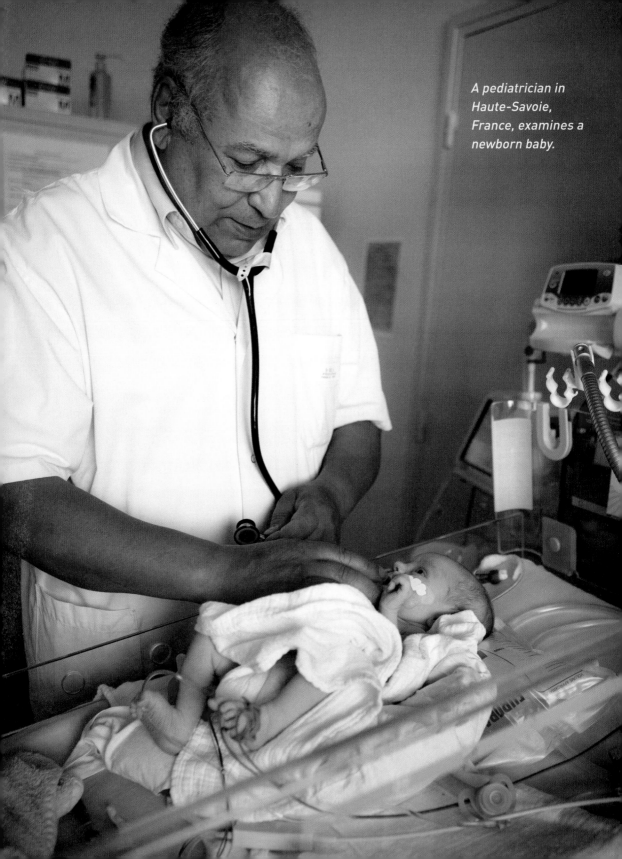

A pediatrician in Haute-Savoie, France, examines a newborn baby.

CHAPTER 1

BASIC HUMAN NEEDS

Words to Understand

Anemia: a condition in which the blood doesn't have enough healthy red blood cells, most often caused by not having enough iron.

Asylum: protection granted by a nation to someone who has left their native country as a political refugee.

Jihad: the struggle or striving to maintain Islam.

Malnutrition: lack of proper nutrition, caused by not having enough to eat, not eating enough of the right things, or being unable to use the food that one does eat.

Mortality rate: a measure of the number of deaths in an area usually within the span of a year.

Countries in Europe in general have the means to meet the basic health and nutrition needs of their people. The northern Scandinavian countries fare best overall, but throughout Europe health and nutrition has been on an upward trend.

The World Health Organization (WHO) says that **malnutrition** in the undernourished may be the gravest single threat to public health worldwide. This lack of sufficient nutrition is the biggest contributor to deaths of children. About six million children die from hunger every year. The most common problem when it comes to lacking nutrients is iron deficiency. Around the world, about half of all preschool children are not getting enough iron—a condition called **anemia**. These children may have health problems later in life, and they often don't do as well in school.

In Europe as in other areas, malnutrition affects the poor most. In the United Kingdom, a group of scientists published an open letter to the prime minister calling for action against this problem. They wrote that there is "a vicious circle . . . with poorer people having worse diets and contributing to the worrying rise in obesity, diabetes and other dietary-related diseases."

Even in a country like Finland that scores high on the SPI, the children in low-income families are more likely to not eat enough fish, breads with fiber, and skimmed milk compared to those who are wealthier.

Lack of proper nutrition can affect older people as well. In the European Union, about 1 in 10 individuals over the age of 65 may be undernourished, and some studies have found that as many as 1 in 3 patients in nursing homes and hospitals are not getting the right nutrition.

Keeping Mothers and Children Alive

Consider maternal mortality. This is the death of women who are pregnant, die in childbirth, or die within a few weeks of the termination of a pregnancy. In most countries throughout Europe, there have been fewer of these maternal deaths over the years. WHO reported that there were 35 such deaths per 100,000 live births in 1990 compared to 16 per 100,000 in 2008.

A hearty cry is a sign of good health in new babies.

Overall, the risk of a child dying before the age of five is low in Europe compared to other areas in the world. WHO estimates that the rate of children dying at this age is about 12 per 1,000 live births in Europe. Compare that number to Africa, where the rate is 90 per 1,000 live births. When looking at the world as a whole, about 17,000 children died every day in 2013. As high as that number seems, it equals 46 deaths per 1,000 live births, which is down from 90 deaths per 1,000 in 1990. The lowest child **mortality rate** in Europe was in Iceland with 2.4 deaths per 1,000 live births. The United Kingdom, which many consider as one of the more economically advanced countries in Europe, ranks number 20—with almost 5 deaths per 1,000 live births.

Infants are much more likely to die when they are raised in poverty or have mothers who smoked or drank during pregnancy. Countries with well-established charity programs to help the poor and food banks have lower child death rates. Many countries in Europe also have social programs established through their government, which help poor families get funding and food to support their children. Social protection programs that help poor families make sure they have safe housing, enough healthy food to eat, and money to buy shoes and clothes for their children help lower child mortality rates.

Clean Water for All

Everyone in the world needs access to clean drinking water. The United Nations calls access to clean water a basic human right. Although access to clean water has increased in Europe over the last 10 years, WHO says that it is still a luxury for many. The organization estimates that 100 million people in this region are unable to get piped water into their homes, and about 19 million cannot get drinking water that is appropriately protected from contaminants. About six million people have to rely on surface water sources such as rivers, streams, ponds, and lakes to get water.

Many of us may also take toilets and sewage systems for granted, but having access to these largely improves the health of people. Again, WHO says that about two million people throughout Europe do not have access to toilets and have to openly defecate in the streets. The poor sanitation leads to health conditions like diarrhea, which can be deadly. About 10 Europeans die every day from diarrhea because of poor sanitation and harmful water sources.

Why Iceland Is Great for Kids' Health

Iceland is the land of volcanoes, geysers, and lagoons of bubbling hot waters. It is also the place in Europe where the fewest children die. One of the reasons for the low mortality rate is accident prevention. Herdís Storgaard, the director of the accident prevention center Forvarnarhús in Iceland, told Iceland magazine *visir.is* that initiatives to prevent accidents have kept many more kids alive. For example, she points to safeguards at public swimming pools. Iceland is a participant in the European Child Safety Alliance and has taken measures to protect children against drownings, falls, traffic accidents, poisonings, and other potential causes of death. All children here also have access to health care. Iceland has a universal health care system in which 85 percent of the citizens' health care is paid for by taxes. Inpatient care in a maternity ward is free of charge. Despite a financial crisis in 2008 and the ruin of the Icelandic banking system, the country is still considered wealthy. The country also has an incredibly clean, green environment, and people tend to eat healthy food. Plus, many citizens spend time in the outdoors, leading to active, healthy adults and children.

Iceland is a great place to grow up—for health and for scenic beauty. Shown here, the snow-covered mountains of Héðinsfjarðargöng in northeast Iceland.

How Garbage Can Lead to a Crisis

Garbage collection is key to a healthy environment. If rotting garbage builds in the streets, it poses a health hazard. Mountains of trash slow how a city operates, and contamination and smells can make people sick. Some cities in Europe have faced repeating waste management problems, where the streets overflow with trash. Athens, Greece, is familiar with the garbage buildup from trash collector strikes. In 2007 a major landfill in Greece reached a saturation point. With no immediate location to dump refuse, garbage piled up and decayed in the streets. Naples, Italy, is notorious for its garbage problems. Dumps and incinerators in Naples have reached their limits several times in recent years. In 2010 tons of garbage were left in the streets for weeks with nowhere to go. Nearby landfills that reached capacity were giving off pollutants that burned eyes and throats. The fumes made people cough and vomit. Some citizens did not open their windows or let their children play outside. Some areas of Naples have reported rising rates of leukemia, throat cancer, and respiratory illnesses. Many believe that increasing pollution is to blame. Many people blamed local mobsters who have controlled garbage collection. The situation has led to violent riots. The garbage crisis declined as newly elected officials came up with plans to get rid of mounting trash, including new incinerators and shipping garbage as far away as the Netherlands.

Naples, Italy—Garbage piles up in the streets of Naples because of a dispute over collection fees.

Berlin, Germany—A man walking his dog in a neglected part of Berlin north of Köpenickerstrasse (Köpenicker Street) close to a former ice factory. The ground is covered with litter and garbage.

Having a Place to Call Home

Housing is another benchmark by which people's well-being is evaluated. While many people do have shelter throughout Europe, a report from Housing Europe ("The State of Housing in the EU 2015") has found that the overall state of housing is unstable. Researchers observed that more people are without a home today in Europe than six years ago, and not enough affordable homes are available in most European countries to meet an increasing demand.

Three overall problems face those who seek a home: rental prices are rising and expensive, home ownership is not affordable due to the extremely high costs, and programs that provide low-cost housing are overwhelmed with high demand. This has led to a phenomenon throughout Europe where many young adults ages 18 to 34 live with their parents. This is the case for two-thirds of the young adults in Italy and three out of four young Slovakian adults. In Portugal and Spain, more than 50 percent of individuals in this age group are living with their parents.

Housing project in United Kingdom, Sheffield.

Affordable housing options exist throughout many European cities, mostly created by nonprofit housing associations. For example, in the seventh-largest city in the Netherlands, Tilburg, just over half of the housing is owned by one housing association, and all this housing is considered to be affordable. These homes rent for one-half to two-thirds of market rate. In London developers are required to have 25 to 35 percent of their newly built units set at an affordable rent. Countries such as Denmark and Austria build "social housing," which is public housing that is financed by the governments. These homes are for lower-class and middle-class families. In 2014 the mayor of Copenhagen, Denmark, Frank Jensen, said that rising property values were swiftly pricing regular wage earners out of the city. To counteract the problem, new legislation has

Migrant refugees at Keleti Railway Station Transit Zone in Budapest, Hungary.

provided for up to one-quarter of future residential buildings to be designated as affordable housing.

In France, many lower-income people (including recent immigrants from Algeria, Morocco, and sub-Saharan Africa) find affordable housing in French suburbs called *banlieues.* In one such banlieue called Sevran outside of Paris, three out of four live in subsidized housing and more than a third live below the poverty level, according to an article in 2013 in *The Economist.* France has struggled with helping recent immigrants fit in and find employment.

Energy services are crucial to human well-being and a country's economic development. Still, around the world about 1.3 billion people have no access to electricity. Europeans, however, are fortunate, with 100% having access to electricity.

Iceland produces almost all the energy it uses with geothermal and hydroelectric plants. Shown here, Krafla Geothermal Power Station, the largest in Iceland, with a distinctive cooling tower reminiscent of a cheese grater.

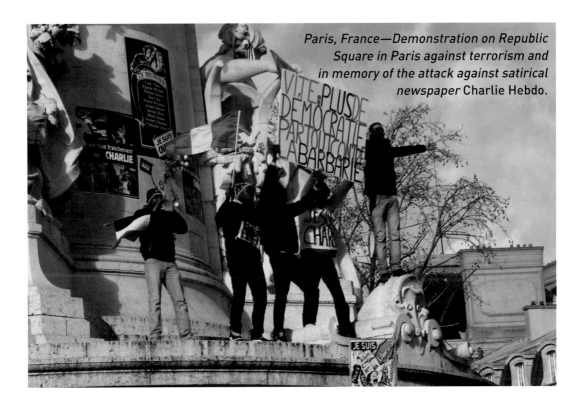

Paris, France—Demonstration on Republic Square in Paris against terrorism and in memory of the attack against satirical newspaper Charlie Hebdo.

Staying Safe

Part of feeling safe is living in an environment without fear of harm or violence. For example, the United States scores low on some points here because its homicide rate has been vastly higher than other Western countries for decades. Central and South America, however, are actually the most murderous regions on earth. Europe has a low rate of gun deaths and a low homicide rate overall.

In general, Europe faces little political unrest. Recently, some European citizens have been targeted with terrorist acts by Islamic extremists. Some who observe the Islamic religion believe in a type of **jihad** to preserve and defend the religion; it does not have to be violent. Some, however, believe that violence is required in instances. In January 2015, Islamic extremists killed political cartoonists in Paris, whom they believed were insulting their religion. On November 13, 2015, terrorists with the Islamic State of Iraq and the Levant (ISIL), also known as ISIS or Daesh, killed 129 people in an attack in Paris. ISIS is a jihadist group with a violent ideology and claims religious authority over all Muslims. In March 2016 suicide bombings at the airport and in the subway in Brussels, Belgium, killed 32 people and wounded over 300. ISIS claimed responsibility for the attacks.

A wave of immigrants fleeing unrest in North Africa and the Middle East has led to conflict between groups of people in Europe. The numbers entering Europe have reached staggering heights, and the whole continent is grappling with finding solutions. Six months into 2015, about 2,000 migrants had drowned in the

Lesvos, Greece—A refugee is given help after being brought ashore by a volunteer lifeguard. A refugee boat and Turkey can be seen in the background.

Mediterranean as they overcrowded boats heading for the coasts of Greece and Italy. In recent years, there has been a surge of desperate migrants from Syria and North Africa hoping to get into Europe. Germany has received the highest number of **asylum** applications in the European Union. An estimated 900,000 refugees entered Germany in 2015.

A few cities are seeing increased drug use, and this is leading to increasing drug-related violence. Marseilles, France, has been plagued by this type of crime. In the Netherlands incidents of violence have erupted over cocaine sales.

Text-Dependent Questions

1. What has the World Health Organization identified as the biggest contributor to deaths of children?
2. In what European country do the fewest children die?
3. Why is garbage removal a measure of well-being?
4. As housing prices rise, how are many young Europeans coping?
5. What is the biggest crisis facing Europe in terms of people?

Research Projects

Considering the great influx of immigrants into Europe, many are interested in how to gain citizenship in Europe. Often citizenship is granted because of (1) descent, (2) marriage, or (3) naturalization. Find out how people can gain citizenship in five different European countries.

A Polish organic farmer has reason to smile—demand is surging, with the national total of organic acreage doubling every three years.

CHAPTER 2

FOUNDATIONS OF WELL-BEING

Words to Understand

Baccalaureate: in Europe, this is an examination intended to qualify successful candidates for higher education.

Biodiversity: the variety of life that is absolutely essential to the health of different ecosystems.

Centenarian: a person who is 100 years old or more.

Greenhouse gas: a gas that contributes to the greenhouse effect by absorbing infrared radiation. The greenhouse effect is the trapping of the sun's warmth in the planet's lower atmosphere due to the greater transparency of atmosphere.

Illiteracy: the inability to read or write.

When it comes to factors that make up a country's well-being, 9 out of the top 10 countries with the best foundations for well-being are in Europe. In 2015 number one was Norway; number two was Switzerland; number three was Sweden; number four was Iceland; and number five was the Netherlands. New Zealand takes the number six spot, and then the final three in the top 10 were Denmark, Finland, and Austria.

It may seem most surprising that Estonia was in the top 10 in 2014 in this category, and still beats out European powerhouses like England, France, and Italy. The country's GDP per capita is modest at $25,132, compared to about $37,000 in France and $64,100 in the United Kingdom. Estonia regained its independence in 1991 after the fall of the Soviet Union. Over the span of two decades, Estonia became a leader in technology, according to *The Economist* magazine. The

Tallinn, Estonia—Crowded street near Town Hall Square in Old Town. Old Tallinn is part of the UNESCO World Heritage site. A thriving town life depends on many important underlying factors.

government equipped all schools with computers. By 1998, all schools were online. In 2000, Estonia declared that access to the Internet is a human right; as a result free WiFi is available almost everywhere in the country. The country has superfast broadband speeds and has cultivated an atmosphere that is pro-technology. In fact, the country holds a record for having the most start-ups per person. These factors have all contributed to the nation's budding prosperity and growth.

Education: An Engine That Can Power Better Lives

The English philosopher and statesman Francis Bacon said, "Knowledge is power." The jazz musician Miles Davis once said, "Knowledge is freedom." Knowledge is an essential building block for people to thrive, survive, and advance, and that's why access to basic knowledge is one of the measures of success to evaluate a country's well-being. The fact is, education empowers people so they can live healthier, more productive, and more rewarding lives.

Illiteracy holds back about one in seven people worldwide but very few Europeans. Globally, the UNESCO Institute for Statistics says that 781 million adults and 126 million youths cannot read or write a simple sentence. According to UNESCO, the literacy rate throughout Europe is at almost 99 percent, which is very high compared to some other parts of the world.

Around the world, more kids are heading into primary school. Enrollment for these youngsters has increased by about 11 percent since 1990. The numbers are very high throughout Europe with 97 to 99 percent primary school enrollment in the United Kingdom, Spain, Netherlands, Finland, Portugal, Iceland, Greece, Sweden, France, Denmark, Slovenia, Italy, and Germany. The European countries with lower rates of primary school enrollment include

Romania and Croatia. Even though lower than in other countries, the primary school enrollment in these nations is still above 85 percent.

Lower secondary school is considered grades five or sixth through eighth. Upper secondary school is usually grades 9 through 12. Again, Europe gets high marks providing public education at these levels with enrollment numbers throughout Europe above 97 percent in most countries.

UNICEF points out that girls continue to suffer a severe disadvantage and exclusion in education systems in many areas around the world. Providing girls with an education helps break the cycle of poverty. Educated women add to a healthy society. Europe does well in providing education to both genders.

Close-up: The French Education System

France is a good example of a functioning educational system in Europe. The majority of schools in France—85 percent—are public and free. Two- to three-year-old toddlers can go to nursery school, where they are introduced to reading, writing, and numbers. From ages 6 to 11, children can attend free primary public schools. From ages 11 to 15, students move on to college, which in France is an equivalent to the early years of high school in the United States. But then between the ages of 15 and 18, the young French adults go to what is called high school. They either attend a *lycée* that leads to earning a specialized degree or baccalaureate, or a professional *lycée* that leads them to a trade or skill and earning a professional baccalaureate. In the traditional "bac" program, students are guided into one of three courses of study that suit their strengths—math and sciences, economics, or languages and literature. In a professional bac program, pupils study specific skills leading to jobs in construction, plumbing, electricity, sales, fashion, or secretarial work, for example. Started under Napoleon in 1808, the baccalaureate is the world's oldest and most famous school leaving exam.

Access to Information

The ability to freely access ideas and information from anywhere in the world is another measure of social progress. The United Nations calls access to the Internet a basic human right because it enables people to "exercise their right to freedom of opinion and expression." The European Union has guidelines on human rights and freedom of expression and it recognizes that the Internet and digital technologies have expanded the possibilities of individuals and media to exercise the right to freedom of expression and freely access online information. Nine of the top 10 countries in this category are in Europe, including Norway, Netherlands, Iceland, Luxembourg, Denmark, Finland, Sweden, Switzerland, and Germany. The Norwegian government has

Stavanger, Norway. Oil capital of Europe. Ironically, oil wealth has greatly eased Norwegians' path to sustainable development—and enhanced material prosperity for the populace.

increasingly focused on Internet access, broadband services and content. In 2010 Finland became the first country in the world to make broadband Internet service a legal right for every citizen.

Live Long and Prosper

Life expectancy is a strong indicator of how healthy a population is. Countries where people live longer must be doing something right. The Social Progress Index for 2015 reports that Japan is in the number one spot in this category. Citizens there live to an average age of about 84 years old. The world's largest percentage of **centenarians** lives on the island of Okinawa. In 2000, there were about 35 people 100 years or older per 100,000 residents. Some say their secret is plenty of outdoor activity and nutritious food. There is an old saying on the island: "Eat until you are 80 percent full."

Many countries in Europe fall in the top ranking as far as living long is concerned. Italy, Iceland, Switzerland, France, and Spain take the numbers 2 through 6 spots. The United States takes the number 30 spot. Some have suggested that Italy fares so well because of healthy lifestyle and diet. The citizens of the Italian island of Sardinia are particularly long lived, with quite a few living beyond 100. Some say the Mediterranean diet—which stresses fish, olive oil, and fresh fruits and vegetables—may contribute. Between 1990 and 2009 the average life expectancy rose by six years throughout the European Union, according to an article in *Lancet*.

Scientists also look at suicide rates to gauge public health. Lithuania, Poland, and Hungary are among the countries with the highest rates. Economic factors are said to contribute to the problem, along with a lack of services for suicide prevention. Greece has had one of the lowest suicide rates in Europe but an article in *The Economist* highlighted how the economic crisis there may have led to more financial despair among its people and to an increase in the suicide rate. Some say that the strong Christian values in that country, however, have kept the suicide rate low.

Shoppers at this market in the Bordeaux region of France can find many healthful, appealing foods.

Europe Packs on the Pounds

Obesity has become one of the greatest public health challenges of the 21st century, and it certainly contributes to mortality rates. The World Health Organization says that the prevalence of obesity in Europe has tripled since the 1980s. Obesity leads to a host of problems, including physical disabilities, psychological issues, and an increased risk of heart disease, cancer, diabetes, and other diseases. The WHO reports that the highest rates of obesity in Western Europe are in the United Kingdom, where one-quarter of all men are pushing the scales beyond the healthy weight zone. The increase in obesity in the UK has led the UN Food and Agriculture Organization to call Great Britain "the fat man of Europe."

"It is no exaggeration to say that it [obesity] is the biggest public health crisis facing the UK today," said Professor Terence Stephenson in "Measuring Up," a 2013 report on the nation's obesity crisis by the Academy of Medical Royal Colleges (AMRC). What is contributing to obesity? Lifestyles that are increasingly sedentary have added on pounds—desk jobs, computers, and TVs have all increased the problem, and it only grows worse because of a higher consumption of high-calorie foods.

Pollution and Premature Death

Public health is also measured by the number of premature deaths. These are deaths that occur before reaching an average expected age, such as 75 or 80. In most of Europe the probability of dying prematurely is lower than in other parts of the world. The World Health Organization reports that one of the largest contributors to premature death in the past few decades has been an increase in air pollution, which has led to more lung and heart disease. When looking at deaths attributable to outdoor air pollution, some of the poorer African countries rank better than Europe because there are simply a lot fewer factories and cars in these countries. The top two European countries that have the best rating in this area are Norway and Iceland. In 2015 the World Health Organization published a paper finding that there were a total of 600,000 premature deaths caused by air pollution in Europe in 2010. The health problems and loss of life from air pollution come at great cost—the WHO estimates that $1.6 trillion was lost in 2010 from this pollution. Cities such as Zurich in Switzerland and Copenhagen in Denmark are enforcing policies to reduce pollutants—restricting the use of diesel cars, trucks, and construction machines. On the other hand, Lisbon in Portugal has few policies in place for combating dirty air.

Many European countries score high when it comes to **greenhouse gas** emissions (meaning their greenhouse emission levels are low in comparison to other countries)—most notably Norway, Switzerland, Sweden, Iceland, Finland, Denmark, Netherlands, United Kingdom, Ireland, Austria, and Germany. Greenhouse gases are those that contribute to global warming.

Water may be something that many wealthier countries take for granted, but fresh water is a concern in all countries. The west coast of the United States, for example, has seen its reservoirs of fresh water greatly decline in recent years. That's why the Social Progress Index also looks at the quantity of water removed from available sources for human use compared to the total volume of water available. The European Union has a Water Framework Directive dedicated to cleaning polluted waters and ensuring that clean waters are kept clean.

"A place for the climate" (Un espace pour le climat) exhibition at France's environment ministry in Paris promotes the Climate Change Conference 2015 (COP21), organized by the French government.

Ecosystems

Biodiversity is the variety of life on earth—this natural diversity makes the planet inhabitable. The European Union is committed to the protection of biodiversity and stopping the loss of biodiversity in the continent by 2020. Switzerland, Germany, Slovenia, Estonia, and Luxembourg all rank very high for maintaining biodiversity. The Environmental Performance Index ranks countries on how well they perform on protection of human health from environmental harm and protection of ecosystems. On their 2014 Index, Switzerland, Luxembourg, Czech Republic, Germany, Spain, Austria, Sweden, Norway, Netherlands, United Kingdom, Denmark, Iceland, Slovenia, Portugal, Finland, Ireland, and Estonia are all in the top 20.

Text-Dependent Questions

1. Although Estonia is a relatively small and poor nation, it has become a leader in what area?
2. Why is education so important to the health of a country?
3. What has been one of the largest, manufactured contributors to premature death is the world?
4. While lack of food has led to increased mortality, a health issue that is almost the opposite has increased deaths worldwide. What is this modern health problem that is causing more deaths?

Research Projects

Find out the details on at least three programs in Europe that are helping to reduce air and water pollution.

Crowds gather in Barcelona, Spain, to support the independence vote of the Spanish region of Catalan.

CHAPTER 3

OPPORTUNITY

Another measure of well-being among citizens is the protection of personal rights. Personal rights pertain to personal security, personal liberty, and private property. On the Social Progress Index, countries of the world have great variance on different measures of opportunity. Some score as high as 98.4 points out of 100 and others score only about 2. These rights include freedom of speech, freedom of movement, and political rights. **Tolerance** and inclusion are also measures of personal rights.

Most countries in Europe show respect for democratic standards and civil liberties and embrace rights for people of all **ethnicities**. However, many face growing nationalist sentiment in response to an influx of immigrants. As people in some countries move into middle-income status, tolerance and inclusion scores often decline before they improve. Some citizens feel that

Support of Personal Rights in the UK

On the Social Progress Index, the United Kingdom ranks almost at the very top when it comes to personal rights—the country is number 3 after New Zealand and Australia. Also, the country takes the number 6 position worldwide when it comes to opportunity. Great Britain champions equality, diversity, and human rights. The government is considered to be relatively free from corruption. The nation has an extensive antibribery act. The press is free to voice all opinions. There are many daily papers and other media driving different perspectives. Freedom of religion is protected. There is no restriction to Internet access. People are free to gather and assemble. Workers can organize. There are large numbers of immigrants living in Britain, but laws are designed to give them equal treatment. There are antidiscrimination laws regarding age, disability, race, religion, sex, and sexual orientation. Women receive equal treatment under the law, but they remain underrepresented in top positions in politics and business, according to Freedom House. The country gets fairly high scores for its tolerance of immigrants and homosexuals. When it comes to religious tolerance and **discrimination** and violence against minorities, however, England ranks in a midrange, so although it is tolerant overall, there have been elevating tensions as more immigrants enter the country.

new immigrants may take away jobs from those who are natives, and these sentiments only grow worse during times of economic stress.

Access to Higher Education

The European Union also does well when it comes to providing a higher education. EU citizens are entitled to subsidized or fully free education at many universities across the continent. Many of the courses are taught in English. Undergraduate

Thousands of students take to the streets in Rome to protest against Prime Minister Matteo Renzi's "the Good School" education reform. They assert the right to education as a basis to demand free education.

A Vote for Gay Marriage in Ireland

On the Social Progress Index, Ireland scores high when it comes to personal rights, personal freedom and choice, and tolerance and inclusion. The country's stand on gay marriage may be one of the best examples of this. In May 2015, Ireland became the first country to legalize same-sex marriage by popular vote. (Some 20 other countries have already legalized gay marriage but not by public vote as in this case.) The citizens of Ireland voted resoundingly in favor of marriage equality with almost two-thirds voting "yes" to a constitutional amendment saying that two people can get married "without distinction as to their sex." The vote was 62 percent in favor and 38 percent opposed. The turnout was one of the largest in the country's history as well. Of more than 3 million possible voters, more than 1.2 million supported gay marriage while 734,300 voted against it.

Many have found this social revolution to be remarkable considering Ireland's long conservative Catholic history. Divorce in Ireland was illegal until 1995, and its legalization depended on a razor-thin margin. Abortion is illegal unless the pregnancy puts the mother's life in danger. Homosexuality was considered a criminal offense by the Irish government up until 1993 when it was officially decriminalized. Laws against homosexuality in the country date back 150 years. In 1861 engaging in homosexual relations was punishable by imprisonment with hard labor. The initial movement toward real reform did not come about until the 1970s when the Campaign for Homosexual Law Reform began. In 1983, Ireland held its first gay pride festival, which also spotlighted violence and intolerance that gays in the country were subject to. In 2010 Ireland passed a Civil Partnership Bill, giving gay couples more rights and legal privileges. In 2013 three openly gay men took seats in the Irish Parliament. In 2015 Leo Varadkar became the first openly gay cabinet member in Ireland. Public attitudes were evolving, and acceptance and tolerance for those in the gay community were growing.

Although the influence of the Roman Catholic Church has waned over the decades, about 85 percent of Ireland's population still identifies as Catholic. Many who belong to the church, however, question some of the Catholic religion's tenets or beliefs— especially after the church has faced scandals over child abuse. The Catholic Church officially opposes gay marriage and the social acceptance of homosexuality and same-sex relationships. The Catholic religion, however, teaches that homosexual persons deserve respect, justice, and care. Although some officials from the Vatican have disapproved of the vote, the most recent pope, Pope Francis, has seemed to soften the traditional Catholic opposition to homosexuality indicating that the Church might tolerate some forms of same-sex unions, although not marriage. When the results of the gay marriage vote came in, Ireland's Prime Minister Enda Kenny proclaimed, "With today's vote, we have disclosed who we are: a generous, compassionate, bold, and joyful people."

Dublin, Ireland—Karla Healion retouches a sign in the shop window in a show of support for gay rights during the country's vote for same-sex marriage.

education is free in Sweden and Germany. Postgraduate courses are free at universities in Finland, Denmark, and Norway. Europe has some of the top-ranked universities globally. Countries that offer a number of high-ranking universities include the United Kingdom in the number-one spot, as well as Sweden, Netherlands, Austria, Germany, Spain, and France. When it comes to equality in the attainment of education for women, some European countries rank high—the Czech Republic is in the number-one spot with the lowest level of inequality. Finland, Germany, Norway, Iceland, and Estonia also rank very high. The European Students Union says that across Europe

Warsaw, Poland—The entrance of Warsaw University,
on Krakowskie Przedmiescie Street.

there have been drives to empower women students and academics, through legislation, through mentoring projects teaming women at different levels of academia, and through incentive-based schemes to encourage faculty attitudes to change.

The general freedom enjoyed by Europeans to freely express their political views figures significantly in their ability to meet their full potential. Pictured, protesters of the General Confederation of Greek Workers demonstrate against job cuts and tax hikes.

Text-Dependent Questions

1. How do economic factors make people less tolerant of immigrants?
2. What was a major obstacle slowing the acceptance of homosexuals in Ireland?
3. What do many colleges in Europe offer that very few US colleges provide?

Research Projects

Colleges in Europe may offer a high quality education at a lower price than in the United States. Find out more about attending a European university. What are some examples of affordable options? What does it take to get into the schools? Give examples. What are some advantages and disadvantages of attending school abroad?

Headquarters of the European Central Bank, which safeguards the value of the euro currency for its 19 member states.

CHAPTER 4

EUROPEAN COUNTRIES AT A GLANCE

AUSTRIA

QUICK STATS

Population: 8,665,550 (July 2015 est.)
Urban Population: 66% of total population (2015)
Comparative Size: about the size of South Carolina; slightly more than two-thirds the size of Pennsylvania
Gross Domestic Product (per capita): $46,600 (2014 est.)
Gross Domestic Product (by sector): agriculture: 1.4%, industry: 28.1%, services: 70.5% (2014 est.)
Government: federal republic
Languages: German (official nationwide) 88.6%, Turkish 2.3%, Serbian 2.2%, Croatian (official in Burgenland) 1.6%, other (includes Slovene, official in South Carinthia, and Hungarian, official in Burgenland) 5.3% (2001 est.)

SOCIAL PROGRESS SNAPSHOT

Social Progress Index: 84.45 (+23.45 above 61 world average)
Basic Human Needs: 95.04 (+26.71 above 68.33 world average)
Foundations of Well-being: 82.53 (+16.08 above 66.45 world average)
Opportunity: 75.77 (+27.54 above 48.23 world average)

Once the center of power for the large Austro-Hungarian Empire, Austria was reduced to a small republic after its defeat in World War I. It was annexed by Nazi Germany in 1938 and subsequently occupied by the Allies in 1945. It wasn't until 1955 that a treaty ended the occupation and recognized Austria's independence. Austria joined the European Union in 1995 and entered the EU Economic and Monetary Union in 1999.

Hot air balloons float high above snowy Bishop's Hat mountain peaks during the annual hot air balloon festival in the ski resort of Filzmoos, Austria.

Follow the index every year at socialprogressimperative.org.
Quick Stats from CIA World Factbook.

EUROPEAN COUNTRIES AT A GLANCE **55**

BELGIUM

QUICK STATS
Population: 8,665,550 (July 2015 est.)
Urban Population: 97.9% of total population
Comparative Size: about the size of Maryland
Gross Domestic Product (per capita): $43,000
Gross Domestic Product (by sector): agriculture 0.8%, industry 21.1%, services 78.1%
Government: federal parliamentary democracy under a constitutional monarchy
Languages: Dutch (official) 60%, French (official) 40%, German (official) less than 1%

SOCIAL PROGRESS SNAPSHOT
Social Progress Index: 82.83 (+21.83 above 61 world average)
Basic Human Needs: 93.73 (+25.40 above 68.33 world average)
Foundations of Well-being: 76.57 (+10.12 above 66.45 world average)
Opportunity: 78.19 (+29.96 above 48.23 world average)

Belgium won independence from the Netherlands in 1830 and was occupied by Germany during World Wars I and II. A member of NATO and the European Union, it has prospered as a modern, technologically advanced European state. In recent years constitutional amendments have granted formal recognition and autonomy to the Dutch-speaking Flemings of the north and the French-speaking Walloons of the south. Its capital, Brussels, is home to numerous international organizations, including the EU and NATO.

BULGARIA

QUICK STATS
Population: 7,186,893
Urban Population: 73.9% of total population
Comparative Size: slightly larger than Tennessee
Gross Domestic Product (per capita): $17,900
Gross Domestic Product (by sector): agriculture 4.9, industry 31.2%, services 63.9%
Government: parliamentary democracy
Languages: Bulgarian (official) 76.8%, Turkish 8.2%, Roma 3.8%

SOCIAL PROGRESS SNAPSHOT
Social Progress Index: 70.19 (+9.19 above 61 world average)
Basic Human Needs: 84.73 (+16.40 above 68.33 world average)
Foundations of Well-being: 69.57 (+3.12 above 66.45 world average)
Opportunity: 56.29 (+8.06 above 48.23 world average)

Two children in traditional Bulgarian costumes.

The Bulgars, a Central Asian Turkic tribe, merged with the local Slavic inhabitants in the late 7th century to form the first Bulgarian state. In succeeding centuries, Bulgaria struggled with the Byzantine Empire to assert its place in the Balkans, but by the end of the 14th century the country was overrun by the Ottoman Turks. Bulgaria became independent from the Ottoman Empire in 1908. Having fought on the losing side in both world wars, Bulgaria fell within the Soviet sphere of influence and became a People's Republic in 1946. Communist domination ended in 1990. The country joined NATO in 2004 and the EU in 2007.

CROATIA

QUICK STATS

Population: 4,464,844 (July 2015 est.)
Urban Population: 59% of total population (2015)
Comparative Size: slightly smaller than West Virginia
Gross Domestic Product (per capita): $20,900 (2014 est.)
Gross Domestic Product (by sector): agriculture 4.5%, industry 26.6%, services 68.9% (2014 est.)
Government: parliamentary democracy
Languages: Croatian (official) 95.6%, Serbian 1.2%, other 3% (including Hungarian, Czech, Slovak, and Albanian), unspecified 0.2% (2011 est.)

SOCIAL PROGRESS SNAPSHOT

Social Progress Index: 73.30 (+12.30 above 61 world average)
Basic Human Needs: 87.49 (+19.16 above 68.33 world average)
Foundations of Well-being: 76.09 (+9.64 above 66.45 world average)
Opportunity: 56.32 (+8.09 above 48.23 world average)

After World War I, Croats, Serbs, and Slovenes formed the country of Yugoslavia. Following World War II, Yugoslavia became a federal Communist state. Although Croatia declared its independence from Yugoslavia in 1991, it took four years of fighting before most occupying Serb armies left Croatian lands, along with a majority of Croatia's ethnic Serb population. The last Serb-held enclave was returned to Croatia in 1998. The country joined NATO in April 2009 and the EU in July 2013.

CYPRUS

QUICK STATS

Population: 1,189,197 (July 2015 est.)
Urban Population: 66.9% of total population (2015)
Comparative Size: about 0.6 times the size of Connecticut
Gross Domestic Product (per capita): $30,800 (2014 est.)
Gross Domestic Product (by sector): agriculture 2.9%, industry 10.5%, services 86.6% (2015 est.)
Government: republic
Languages: Greek (official) 80.9%, Turkish (official) 0.2%, English 4.1%, Romanian 2.9%, Russian 2.5%, Bulgarian 2.2%, Arabic 1.2%, Filipino 1.1%, other 4.3%, unspecified 0.6% (2011 est.)

SOCIAL PROGRESS SNAPSHOT

Social Progress Index: 77.45 (+16.45 above 61 world average)
Basic Human Needs: 89.30 (+20.97 above 68.33 world average)
Foundations of Well-being: 75.95 (+9.50 above 66.45 world average)
Opportunity: 67.11 (+18.88 above 48.23 world average)

A former British colony, Cyprus became independent in 1960. Tensions between the Greek Cypriot majority and Turkish Cypriot minority came to a head in December 1963, and in 1983 the Turkish Cypriot–administered area declared itself the Turkish Republic of Northern Cyprus, but it is recognized only by Turkey. In 2004 the entire island entered the EU, but the EU did not recognize the Turkish Cypriot area (although these citizens may get EU privileges).

People arrive at the Olsany Cemetery to mark All Souls' Day in Prague, Czech Republic. All Souls' Day is a Christian festival mainly celebrated by Catholics to remember the dead. People visit the graves of loved ones and place candles and flowers.

CZECH REPUBLIC

QUICK STATS

Population: 10,644,842 (July 2015 est.)
Urban Population: 73% of total population (2015)
Comparative Size: slightly smaller than South Carolina
Gross Domestic Product (per capita): $29,900 (2014 est.)
Gross Domestic Product (by sector): agriculture 2.6%, industry 37.4% services 60% (2014 est.)
Government: parliamentary democracy
Languages: Czech (official) 95.4%, Slovak 1.6%, other 3% (2011 census)

SOCIAL PROGRESS SNAPSHOT

Social Progress Index: 80.59 (+19.59 above 61 world average)
Basic Human Needs: 94.23 (+25.90 above 68.33 world average)
Foundations of Well-being: 79.04 (+12.59 above 66.45 world average)
Opportunity: 68.49 (+20.26 above 48.23 world average)

After World War I Czechs and Slovaks merged to form Czechoslovakia. During World War II Nazi Germany occupied territory that comprises the Czech Republic, and Slovakia allied with Germany. After the war a reunited Czechoslovakia fell under Soviet influence. The peaceful "Velvet Revolution" swept the Communist Party from power in 1989, and democratic rule returned. In 1993 the country separated again into the Czech Republic and Slovakia. The Czech Republic joined NATO in 1999 and the European Union in 2004.

DENMARK

QUICK STATS
Population: 5,581,503 (July 2015 est.)
Urban Population: 87.7% of total population (2015)
Comparative Size: slightly less than twice the size of Massachusetts
Gross Domestic Product (per capita): $44,300 (2014 est.)
Gross Domestic Product (by sector): agriculture 1.3%, industry 21.2%, services 77.5% (2014 est.)
Government: constitutional monarchy
Languages: Danish, Faroese, Greenlandic (an Inuit dialect), German (small minority). Note: English is the predominant second language.

SOCIAL PROGRESS SNAPSHOT
Social Progress Index: 86.63 (+25.63 above 61 world average)
Basic Human Needs: 96.03 (+27.70 above 68.33 world average)
Foundations of Well-being: 82.63 (+16.18 above 66.45 world average)
Opportunity: 81.23 (+33.00 above 48.23 world average)

Once the seat of Viking raiders and later a major northern European power, Denmark has evolved into a modern, prosperous nation that is participating in the general political and economic integration of Europe. It joined NATO in 1949 and the EEC (now the EU) in 1973. However, the country has opted out of certain elements of the European Economic and Monetary Union, European defense cooperation, and issues concerning certain justice and home affairs.

ESTONIA

QUICK STATS
Population: 1,265,420 (July 2015 est.)
Urban Population: 87.5% of total population (2015)
Comparative Size: slightly smaller than New Hampshire and Vermont combined
Gross Domestic Product (per capita): $27,000 (2014 est.)
Gross Domestic Product (by sector): agriculture 3.6%, industry 29.2%, services 67.2% (2014 est.)
Government: parliamentary republic
Languages: Estonian (official) 68.5%, Russian 29.6%, Ukrainian 0.6%, other 1.2%, unspecified 0.1% (2011 est.)

SOCIAL PROGRESS SNAPSHOT
Social Progress Index: 80.49 (+19.49 above 61 world average)
Basic Human Needs: 88.44 (+20.11 above 68.33 world average)
Foundations of Well-being: 79.61 (+13.16 above 66.45 world average)
Opportunity: 73.42 (+25.19 above 48.23 world average)

After centuries of Danish, Swedish, German, and Russian rule, Estonia attained independence in 1918. Forcibly incorporated into the USSR in 1940—an action never recognized by the United States—it regained its freedom in 1991 with the collapse of the Soviet Union. Since 1994 Estonia has been free to promote economic and political ties with the West. It joined both NATO and the EU in the spring of 2004 and adopted the euro as its official currency in 2011.

FINLAND

QUICK STATS

Population: 5,476,922 (July 2015 est.)
Urban Population: 84.2% of total population (2015)
Comparative Size: slightly more than two times the size of Georgia; slightly smaller than Montana
Gross Domestic Product (per capita): $40,300 (2014 est.)
Gross Domestic Product (by sector): agriculture 2.7%, industry 27%, services 70.3% (2014 est.)
Government: republic
Languages: Finnish (official) 89%, Swedish (official) 5.3%, Russian 1.3%, other 4.4% (2014 est.)

SOCIAL PROGRESS SNAPSHOT

Social Progress Index: 86.75 (+25.75 above 61 world average)
Basic Human Needs: 95.05 (+26.72 above 68.33 world average)
Foundations of Well-being: 82.58 (+16.13 above 66.45 world average)
Opportunity: 82.63 (+34.40 above 48.23 world average)

Reindeer raised for their milk feed on moss from their paddock on a farm in Kuusamo, Finland.

Sweden ruled Finland from the 12th through the 19th centuries, and Finland became an autonomous grand duchy of Russia after 1809. It gained complete independence in 1917. During World War II Finland cooperated with Germany, then resisted invasions by the Soviet Union. Finland has transformed from a farm economy to an industrial economy; per capita income is high. An EU member since 1995, Finland has high-quality education, promotion of equality, and a national social welfare system—currently challenged by an aging population and export-driven economy.

FRANCE

QUICK STATS

Population: 66,553,766. Note: This figure is for metropolitan France and five overseas regions; the metropolitan France population is 62,814,233 (July 2015 est.)
Urban Population: 79.5% of total population (2015)
Comparative Size: slightly more than four times the size of Georgia; slightly less than the size of Texas
Gross Domestic Product (per capita): $40,400 (2014 est.)
Gross Domestic Product (by sector): agriculture 1.7%, industry 19.4%, services 78.9% (2014 est.)
Government: republic
Language: French (official) 100%

SOCIAL PROGRESS SNAPSHOT

Social Progress Index: 80.82 (+19.82 above 61 world average)
Basic Human Needs: 91.16 (+22.83 above 68.33 world average)
Foundations of Well-being: 78.83 (+12.38 above 66.45 world average)
Opportunity: 72.46 (+24.23 above 48.23 world average)

One of the most modern countries, France plays an influential role as a member of the United Nations Security Council, NATO, the G-8, the G-20, and the EU. Since 1958 it has constructed a stable hybrid presidential-parliamentary governing system. In recent decades its cooperation with Germany has proved central to the economic integration of Europe. In the early 21st century, five French overseas entities—French Guiana, Guadeloupe, Martinique, Mayotte, and Réunion—were made part of France proper.

GERMANY

QUICK STATS

Population: 80,854,408 (July 2015 est.)
Urban Population: 75.3% of total population (2015)
Comparative Size: three times the size of Pennsylvania; slightly smaller than Montana
Gross Domestic Product (per capita): $45,900 (2014 est.)
Gross Domestic Product (by sector): agriculture 0.9%, industry 30.8%, services 68.4%
Government: federal republic
Language: German (official) 100%

SOCIAL PROGRESS SNAPSHOT

Social Progress Index: 84.04 (+23.04 above 61 world average)
Basic Human Needs: 94.12 (+25.79 above 68.33 world average)
Foundations of Well-being: 81.50 (+15.05 above 66.45 world average)
Opportunity: 76.49 (+28.26 above 48.23 world average)

After two devastating world wars in the 20th century, Germany was occupied by Allied powers in 1945. In 1949 two states were formed: the democratic Federal Republic of Germany (FRG) aligned with key Western organizations (the EC, which became the EU, and NATO), while the Communist German Democratic Republic (GDR) aligned with the Soviet Union. The decline of the USSR led to German reunification in 1990. In January 1999 Germany and 10 other countries introduced a common European currency, the euro.

GREECE

QUICK STATS

Population: 10,775,643 (July 2015 est.)
Urban Population: 78% of total population (2015)
Comparative Size: slightly smaller than Alabama
Gross Domestic Product (per capita): $25,900 (2014 est.)
Gross Domestic Product (by sector): agriculture 3.5%, industry 15.9%, services 80.6% (2014 est.)
Government: parliamentary republic
Languages: Greek (official) 99%, other (includes English and French) 1%

SOCIAL PROGRESS SNAPSHOT

Social Progress Index: 74.03 (+13.03 above 61 world average)
Basic Human Needs: 87.64 (+19.31 above 68.33 world average)
Foundations of Well-being: 74.53 (+8.08 above 66.45 world average)
Opportunity: 59.91 (+11.68 above 48.23 world average)

After achieving independence from the Ottoman Empire in 1830, Greece gradually added neighboring islands and territories. Following German occupation in World War II, Greece entered a protracted civil war between supporters of the king and rebels. Following the rebels' defeat in 1949, Greece joined NATO. In 1967 military officers seized power and suspended many liberties. In 1974 democratic elections created a parliamentary republic. In 1981 Greece joined the EC (now the EU). Since 2010 possible Greek default on euro-denominated debt has created severe strains.

Central Europe's largest arts festival, Sziget draws more than 200 artists from almost 50 countries to Obuda Island on the Danube River near Budapest, Hungary.

HUNGARY

QUICK STATS

Population: 9,897,541 (July 2015 est.)
Urban Population: 71.2% of total population (2015)
Comparative Size: slightly smaller than Virginia; about the same size as Indiana
Gross Domestic Product (per capita): $24,900 (2014 est.)
Gross Domestic Product (by sector): agriculture 3.4%, industry 31.1%, services 65.5% (2014 est.)
Government: parliamentary democracy
Languages: Hungarian (official) 99.6%, English 16%, German 11.2%, Russian 1.6%, Romanian 1.3%, French 1.2%, other 4.2%

SOCIAL PROGRESS SNAPSHOT

Social Progress Index: 74.80 (+13.80 above 61 world average)
Basic Human Needs: 88.80 (+20.47 above 68.33 world average)
Foundations of Well-being: 70.40 (+3.95 above 66.45 world average)
Opportunity: 65.21 (+16.98 above 48.23 world average)

For centuries Hungary served as a bulwark against Ottoman Turkish expansion. The kingdom eventually became part of the Austro-Hungarian Empire, which collapsed during World War I. The country fell under Communist rule following World War II. In 1956 a revolt met with a massive military intervention by Moscow. Under Janos Kadar's leadership in 1968, Hungary began liberalizing its economy. Hungary held multiparty elections in 1990 and initiated a free market economy. It joined NATO in 1999 and the EU five years later.

ICELAND

QUICK STATS

Population: 331,918 (July 2015 est.)
Urban Population: 94.1% of total population (2015)
Comparative Size: slightly smaller than Pennsylvania; about the same size as Kentucky
Gross Domestic Product (per capita): $43,600 (2014 est.)
Gross Domestic Product (by sector): agriculture 6%, industry 22.4%, services 71.7% (2014 est.)
Government: constitutional republic
Languages: Icelandic, English, Nordic languages, German widely spoken

SOCIAL PROGRESS SNAPSHOT

Social Progress Index: 87.62 (+26.62 above 61 world average)
Basic Human Needs: 95.00 (+26.67 above 68.33 world average)
Foundations of Well-being: 86.11 (+19.66 above 66.45 world average)
Opportunity: 81.73 (+33.50 above 48.23 world average)

Iceland boasts the world's oldest-functioning legislative assembly, the Althing, established in 930. Independent for over 300 years, Iceland was subsequently ruled by Norway and Denmark. Fallout from the Askja volcano of 1875 devastated the country. Denmark granted limited home rule in 1874 and complete independence in 1944. The 20th century brought substantial economic growth driven primarily by fishing. The economy has diversified greatly, but Iceland was hard hit by the global financial crisis after 2008. Literacy, longevity, and social cohesion are first rate.

IRELAND

QUICK STATS

Population: 4,892,305 (July 2015 est.)
Urban Population: 63.2% of total population (2015)
Comparative Size: slightly larger than West Virginia
Gross Domestic Product (per capita): $49,200 (2014 est.)
Gross Domestic Product (by sector): agriculture 1.6%, industry 27%, services 71.4% (2014 est.)
Government: republic parliamentary democracy
Languages: English (official, the language generally used), Irish (Gaelic or Gaeilge) (official, spoken by approximately 38.7% of the population as a first or second language in 2011; mainly spoken in areas along the western coast)

SOCIAL PROGRESS SNAPSHOT

Social Progress Index: 84.66 (+23.66 above 61 world average)
Basic Human Needs: 93.68 (+25.35 above 68.33 world average)
Foundations of Well-being: 76.34 (+9.89 above 66.45 world average)
Opportunity: 83.97 (+35.74 above 48.23 world average)

Ireland's history is marked by seven centuries of Anglo-Irish struggle. The Irish famine of the 1800s saw the population drop by one-third. It began growing again in the 1960s, resulting in one of the youngest populations in the EU. In 1998 a phase of cooperation between the Irish and British governments started. The boom years of the "Celtic Tiger" (1995–2007) saw rapid economic growth until the meltdown of the Irish banking system in 2008. Today the economy is recovering.

ITALY

QUICK STATS

Population: 61,855,120 (July 2015 est.)
Urban Population: 69% of total population (2015)
Comparative Size: almost twice the size of Georgia; slightly larger than Arizona
Gross Domestic Product (per capita): $35,500 (2014 est.)
Gross Domestic Product (by sector): agriculture 2.2%, industry 23.9%, services 73.9% (2014 est.)
Government: republic
Languages: Italian (official), German (parts of Trentino-Alto Adige region are predominantly German-speaking), French (small French-speaking minority in Valle d'Aosta region), Slovene (Slovene-speaking minority in the Trieste-Gorizia area)

SOCIAL PROGRESS SNAPSHOT

Social Progress Index: 77.38 (+16.38 above 61 world average)
Basic Human Needs: 88.39 (+20.06 above 68.33 world average)
Foundations of Well-being: 77.00 (+10.55 above 66.45 world average)
Opportunity: 66.76 (+18.53 above 48.23 world average)

Italy became a nation-state in 1861, when King Victor Emmanuel II united regions of the peninsula, along with Sardinia and Sicily. An era of parliamentary government ended in the 1920s with Benito Mussolini's dictatorship. After Italy's defeat in World War II, a democratic republic was established in 1946, and economic revival followed. Italy is a member of NATO and the European Economic Community. Persistent problems include sluggish economic growth, high youth and female unemployment, and organized crime and corruption.

LATVIA

QUICK STATS

Population: 1,986,705 (July 2015 est.)
Urban Population: 67.4% of total population (2015)
Comparative Size: slightly larger than West Virginia
Gross Domestic Product (per capita): $23,700 (2014 est.)
Gross Domestic Product (by sector): agriculture 4.8%, industry 24.8%, services 70.4% (2014 est.)
Government: parliamentary democracy
Languages: Latvian (official) 56.3%, Russian 33.8%, other 0.6% (includes Polish, Ukrainian, and Belarusian), unspecified 9.4%. Note: Percentages represent language usually spoken at home (2011 est.).

SOCIAL PROGRESS SNAPSHOT

Social Progress Index: 74.12 (+13.12 above 61 world average)
Basic Human Needs: 83.84 (+15.51 above 68.33 world average)
Foundations of Well-being: 77.76 (+11.31 above 66.45 world average)
Opportunity: 60.75 (+12.52 above 48.23 world average)

With its name originating from a Baltic tribe, Latvia has been controlled by Germans, Poles, Swedes, and Russians. A Latvian republic emerged following World War I, but the USSR annexed it in 1940—an action never recognized by the United States. Latvia reestablished independence in 1991 following the Soviet Union collapse but retains a Russian minority of about 28%. Latvia joined NATO and the EU in the spring of 2004 and the eurozone in 2014.

LITHUANIA

Students' first-ever day of school in Vilnius, Lithuania.

QUICK STATS

Population: 2,884,433
Urban Population: 66.5% of total population (2015)
Comparative Size: slightly larger than West Virginia
Gross Domestic Product (per capita): $27,100 (2014 est.)
Gross Domestic Product (by sector): agriculture 7.9%, industry 19.6%, services 72.5% (2012 est.)
Government: parliamentary democracy
Languages: Lithuanian (official) 82%, Russian 8%, Polish 5.6%, other 0.9%, unspecified 3.5% (2011 est.)

SOCIAL PROGRESS SNAPSHOT

Social Progress Index: 74.00 (+13.00 above 61 world average)
Basic Human Needs: 83.75 (+15.42 above 68.33 world average)
Foundations of Well-being: 74.79 (+8.34 above 66.45 world average)
Opportunity: 63.47 (+15.24 above 48.23 world average)

By 1400 Lithuania was the largest state in Europe. An alliance with Poland in 1386 led to a union under one ruler, and in 1569 the countries formally united. By 1795 surrounding countries had partitioned the country. Lithuania regained independence following World War I, but the USSR annexed it in 1940. In 1990 Lithuania became the first Soviet republic to declare independence. Lithuania subsequently restructured its economy for Western European integration; it joined NATO and the EU in 2004.

LUXEMBOURG

QUICK STATS

Population: 570,252 (July 2015 est.)
Urban Population: 90.2% of total population (2015)
Comparative Size: slightly smaller than Rhode Island
Gross Domestic Product (per capita): $92,000 (2014 est.)
Gross Domestic Product (by sector): agriculture 0.3%, industry 12%, services 87.7% (2014 est.)
Government: constitutional monarchy
Language(s): Luxembourgish (official administrative language and spoken national language 88.8%, French (official administrative language) 4.2%, Portuguese 2.3%, German (official administrative language) 1.1%, other 3.5% (2011 est.)

SOCIAL PROGRESS SNAPSHOT

Foundations of Well-being: 82.42 (+15.97 above 66.45 world average)
Opportunity: 81.95 (+33.72 above 48.23 world average)
(Not all scores computed due to data gaps in statistical sources.)

Founded in 963, Luxembourg became a grand duchy in 1815 and an independent state under the Netherlands. It lost more than half of its territory to Belgium in 1839 but gained full independence by 1867. Overrun by Germany in both world wars, it ended its neutrality in 1948 when it entered into the Benelux Customs Union and joined NATO the following year. Luxembourg was a founding member of the European Economic Community (later the European Union).

MALTA

A Maltese knight

QUICK STATS
Population: 413,965 (July 2015 est.)
Urban Population: 95.4% of total population (2015)
Comparative Size: slightly less than twice the size of Washington, DC
Gross Domestic Product (per capita): $33,200 (2014 est.)
Gross Domestic Product (by sector): agriculture 1.1%, industry 23.7%, services 75.2% (2014 est.)
Government: republic
Languages: Maltese (official) 90.1%, English (official) 6%, multilingual 3%, other 0.9% (2005 est.)

SOCIAL PROGRESS SNAPSHOT
Foundations of Well-being: 73.61 (+7.16 above 66.45 world average)
Opportunity: 70.38 (+22.15 above 48.23 world average)
(Not all scores computed due to data gaps in statistical sources.)

Great Britain acquired possession of Malta in 1814. The island supported England through both world wars and remained in the Commonwealth when it became independent in 1964; it became a republic a decade later. The island has transformed itself into a freight transshipment point, a financial center, and a tourist destination, while its key industries moved toward more service-oriented activities. Malta became an EU member in May 2004 and began using the euro in 2008.

NETHERLANDS

QUICK STATS
Population: 16,947,904 (July 2015 est.)
Urban Population: 90.5% of total population (2015)
Comparative Size: slightly less than twice the size of New Jersey
Gross Domestic Product (per capita): $47,400 (2014 est.)
Gross Domestic Product (by sector): agriculture 2.8%, industry 22.3%, services 74.8% (2014 est.)
Government: constitutional monarchy
Languages: Dutch (official)

SOCIAL PROGRESS SNAPSHOT
Social Progress Index: 86.50 (+25.50 above 61 world average)
Basic Human Needs: 94.80 (+26.47 above 68.33 world average)
Foundations of Well-being: 83.81 (+17.36 above 66.45 world average)
Opportunity: 80.88 (+32.65 above 48.23 world average)

The Dutch United Provinces declared independence from Spain in 1579; during the 1600s they became a leading commercial power, with colonies around the world. After a 20-year French occupation, a Kingdom of the Netherlands was formed in 1815. In 1830 Belgium seceded. The Netherlands remained neutral in World War I but suffered German occupation in World War II. A modern, industrialized nation, the Netherlands also exports agricultural products. The country helped to found NATO and the EEC (now the EU).

People enjoy the traditional ice skating rink outside the Rijsksmuseum at Museum Square in Amsterdam, Netherlands.

NORWAY

QUICK STATS

Population: 5,207,689 (July 2015 est.)
Urban Population: 80.5% of total population (2015)
Comparative Size: slightly larger than New Mexico
Gross Domestic Product (per capita): $66,900 (2014 est.)
Gross Domestic Product (by sector): agriculture 1.7%, industry 41.8%, services 56.5% (2014 est.)
Government: constitutional monarchy
Languages: Norwegian (official)

SOCIAL PROGRESS SNAPSHOT

Social Progress Index: 88.36 (+27.36 above 61 world average)
Basic Human Needs: 94.80 (+26.47 above 68.33 world average)
Foundations of Well-being: 88.46 (+22.01 above 66.45 world average)
Opportunity: 81.82 (+33.59 above 48.23 world average)

Viking raids into Europe declined with the rise of Christianity in the 10th century. In 1397 Norway entered a four-century union with Denmark. In 1814 Norwegians resisted cession to Sweden and adopted a constitution. Sweden invaded Norway, but it regained independence in 1905. Nazi Germany occupied a neutral Norway, but it abandoned neutrality in 1949 and joined NATO. Discovery of oil and gas in the 1960s boosted the economy. Norway rejected joining the EU and faces issues concerning its social safety net and economic competitiveness.

POLAND

QUICK STATS

Population: 38,562,189 (July 2015 est.)
Urban Population: 60.5% of total population (2015)
Comparative Size: slightly smaller than New Mexico
Gross Domestic Product (per capita): $25,100 (2014 est.)
Gross Domestic Product (by sector): agriculture 3.7%, industry 32%, services 64.3% (2014 est.)
Government: republic
Languages: Polish (official) 98.2%, Silesian 1.4%, other 1.1%, unspecified 1.3%

SOCIAL PROGRESS SNAPSHOT

Social Progress Index: 77.98 (+16.98 above 61 world average)
Basic Human Needs: 86.67 (+18.34 above 68.33 world average)
Foundations of Well-being: 77.19 (+10.74 above 66.45 world average)
Opportunity: 70.07 (+21.84 above 48.23 world average)

By the mid-16th century, the Polish-Lithuanian Commonwealth was vast. During the 1900s, however, Russia, Prussia, and Austria partitioned Poland. It regained independence in 1918 but was overrun by Germany and the Soviet Union in World War II. Labor turmoil in 1980 led to the formation of the independent trade union Solidarity, which became a strong political force. In free elections (1989–1990), Solidarity won parliament and the presidency, closing the Communist era and leading to a robust economy. Poland joined NATO (1999) and the European Union (2004).

PORTUGAL

QUICK STATS

Population: 10,825,309 (July 2015 est.)
Urban Population: 63.5% of total population (2015)
Comparative Size: slightly smaller than New Mexico
Gross Domestic Product (per capita): $27,000 (2014 est.)
Gross Domestic Product (by sector): agriculture 2.6%, industry 22.4%, services 75% (2014 est.)
Government: republic parliamentary democracy
Languages: Portuguese (official), Mirandese (official, but locally used)

SOCIAL PROGRESS SNAPSHOT

Social Progress Index: 81.91 (+20.91 above 61 world average)
Basic Human Needs: 92.81 (+24.48 above 68.33 world average)
Foundations of Well-being: 76.17 (+9.72 above 66.45 world average)
Opportunity: 76.76 (+28.53 above 48.23 world average)

A global maritime power (1400s–1500s), Portugal lost wealth and status with the destruction of Lisbon in a 1755 earthquake, occupation during the Napoleonic Wars, and the independence of Brazil, its wealthiest colony, in 1822. A 1910 revolution deposed the monarchy; for about 60 years, repressive governments ran the country. In 1974 a left-wing military coup installed broad democratic reforms, and Portugal granted independence to its African colonies. Portugal is a member of NATO and the EU.

ROMANIA

QUICK STATS

Population: 21,666,350 (July 2015 est.)
Urban Population: 54.6% of total population (2015)
Comparative Size: slightly smaller than Oregon
Gross Domestic Product (per capita): $19,700 (2014 est.)
Gross Domestic Product (by sector): agriculture 5.4%, industry 27.3%, services 67.3% (2014 est.)
Government: republic
Languages: Romanian (official) 85.4%, Hungarian 6.3%, Romany (Gypsy) 1.2%, other 1%, unspecified 6.1% (2011 est.)

SOCIAL PROGRESS SNAPSHOT

Social Progress Index: 68.37 (+7.37 above 61 world average)
Basic Human Needs: 77.35 (+9.02 above 68.33 world average)
Foundations of Well-being: 71.53 (+5.08 above 66.45 world average)
Opportunity: 56.24 (+8.01 above 48.23 world average)

Romanian traditional Easter eggs

Under Turkish Ottoman rule for centuries, Wallachia and Moldavia united in 1862 as Romania. The country joined the Allied Powers in World War I and acquired Transylvania. In 1941 Romania joined the German invasion of the USSR. Three years later, Soviets overran Romania, leading to a Communist "people's republic." The dictator Nicolae Ceausescu's oppressive rule lasted from 1965 until his overthrow in the 1980s. Former Communists dominated until 1996, when they were swept from power. Romania joined NATO (2004) and the EU (2007).

SLOVAKIA

QUICK STATS
Population: 5,445,027 (July 2015 est.)
Urban Population: 53.6% of total population (2015)
Comparative Size: about twice the size of New Hampshire
Gross Domestic Product (per capita): $28,200 (2014 est.)
Gross Domestic Product (by sector): agriculture 3.4%, industry 22.5%, services 74.1% (2014 est.)
Government: parliamentary democracy
Languages: Slovak (official) 78.6%, Hungarian 9.4%, Roma 2.3%, Ruthenian 1%, other or unspecified 8.8% (2011 est.)

SOCIAL PROGRESS SNAPSHOT
Social Progress Index: 78.45 (+17.45 above 61 world average)
Basic Human Needs: 92.19 (+23.86 above 68.33 world average)
Foundations of Well-being: 78.80 (+12.35 above 66.45 world average)
Opportunity: 64.35 (+16.12 above 48.23 world average)

In 1867 Slovaks were living under the Austro-Hungarian monarchy. Policies favoring the use of the Hungarian language strengthened Slovak nationalism and ties with related Czechs. After the Austro-Hungarian Empire dissolved, Slovaks formed Czechoslovakia with Czechs. In 1939 Slovakia became an independent state allied with Nazi Germany. Following World War II, Czechoslovakia was reconstituted and came under Communist rule. Communists were peacefully swept from power in 1989, and democratic rule began. In 1993 Slovakia and the Czech Republic formed. Slovakia joined NATO and the EU in 2004.

SLOVENIA

QUICK STATS
Population: 1,983,412 (July 2015 est.)
Urban Population: 49.6% of total population (2015)
Comparative Size: slightly smaller than New Jersey
Gross Domestic Product (per capita): $29,700 (2014 est.)
Gross Domestic Product (by sector): agriculture 2.1%, industry 28.4%, services 69.5% (2014 est.)
Government: parliamentary republic
Languages: Slovenian (official) 91.1%, Serbo-Croatian 4.5%, other or unspecified 4.4%, Italian (official, only in municipalities where Italian national communities reside), Hungarian (official, only in municipalities where Hungarian national communities reside) (2002 census)

SOCIAL PROGRESS SNAPSHOT
Social Progress Index: 81.62 (+20.62 above 61 world average)
Basic Human Needs: 92.88 (+24.55 above 68.33 world average)
Foundations of Well-being: 80.87 (+14.42 above 66.45 world average)
Opportunity: 71.12 (+22.89 above 48.23 world average)

With the breakup of the Austro-Hungarian Empire following World War I, Slovenes joined Serbs and Croats in forming a multinational state, named Yugoslavia, in 1929. After World War II, Slovenia became a Communist republic but distanced itself from Moscow. Dissatisfied by majority Serbs, Slovenes established independence in 1991 after a short 10-day war. With a strong economy and a stable democracy, Slovenia transformed into a modern state. Slovenia joined NATO and the EU in 2004.

Spain

QUICK STATS

Population: 48,146,134 (July 2015 est.)
Urban Population: 79.6% of total population (2015)
Comparative Size: almost five times the size of Kentucky; slightly more than twice the size of Oregon
Gross Domestic Product (per capita): $33,700 (2014 est.)
Gross Domestic Product (by sector): agriculture 3.2%, industry 25.4%, services 71.4% (2014 est.)
Government: parliamentary monarchy
Languages: Castilian Spanish (official) 74%, Catalan 17%, Galician 7%, Basque 2%

SOCIAL PROGRESS SNAPSHOT

Social Progress Index: 81.17 (+20.17 above 61 world average)
Basic Human Needs: 91.09 (+22.76 above 68.33 world average)
Foundations of Well-being: 76.79 (+10.34 above 66.45 world average)
Opportunity: 75.62 (+27.39 above 48.23 world average)

Spain's powerful world empire (1500s–1600s) ultimately yielded command of the seas to England. Subsequent failure to embrace the industrial revolution caused the country to fall behind Britain, France, and Germany. Spain remained neutral in World Wars I and II but suffered through a devastating civil war (1936–1939). After the death of the dictator Francisco Franco in 1975, Spain transitioned to democracy and modernized (joining the EU in 1986). More recently the government has focused on reversing an economic recession that began in mid-2008.

Sweden

QUICK STATS

Population: 9,801,616 (July 2015 est.)
Urban Population: 85.8% of total population (2015)
Comparative Size: slightly larger than California
Gross Domestic Product (per capita): $46,000 (2014 est.)
Gross Domestic Product (by sector): agriculture 1.8%, industry 33.4%, services 64.8% (2014 est.)
Government: constitutional monarchy
Languages: Swedish (official), small Sami- and Finnish-speaking minorities

SOCIAL PROGRESS SNAPSHOT

Social Progress Index: 88.06 (+27.06 above 61 world average)
Basic Human Needs: 94.83 (+26.50 above 68.33 world average)
Foundations of Well-being: 86.43 (+19.98 above 66.45 world average)
Opportunity: 82.93 (+34.70 above 48.23 world average)

Vikings laid the 1,500-year-old Ale's Stones monument in the shape of a ship on the Baltic Sea coast in Kaseberga, Sweden.

A military power during the 17th century, Sweden has not participated in any war for two centuries. An armed neutrality was preserved in both world wars. Sweden's long-successful economic formula of a capitalist system with welfare elements was challenged in the 1990s by high unemployment and by the global economic downturns in the following decade. Sweden joined the EU in 1995, but the public rejected the introduction of the euro in a 2003 referendum.

SWITZERLAND

QUICK STATS
Population: 8,121,830 (July 2015 est.)
Urban Population: 73.9% of total population (2015)
Comparative Size: slightly less than twice the size of New Jersey
Gross Domestic Product (per capita): $46,000 (2014 est.)
Gross Domestic Product (by sector): agriculture 1.8%, industry 33.4%, services 64.8% (2014 est.)
Government: formally a confederation but similar in structure to a federal republic
Languages: German (official) 64.9%, French (official) 22.6%, Italian (official) 8.3%, Serbo-Croatian 2.5%, Albanian 2.6%, Portuguese 3.4%, Spanish 2.2%, English 4.6%, Romansch (official) 0.5%, other 5.1%

SOCIAL PROGRESS SNAPSHOT
Social Progress Index: 87.97 (+26.97 above 61 world average)
Basic Human Needs: 95.66 (+27.33 above 68.33 world average)
Foundations of Well-being: 86.50 (+20.05 above 66.45 world average)
Opportunity: 81.75 (+33.52 above 48.23 world average)

A constitution of 1848, modified in 1874, created a centralized Swiss federal government. Switzerland's sovereignty and neutrality have long been honored by the major European powers, and the country was not involved in the two world wars. The political and economic integration of Europe over the past half century, as well as Switzerland's role in many UN and international organizations, has strengthened Switzerland's ties with its neighbors. However, Switzerland did not become a UN member until 2002.

UNITED KINGDOM

QUICK STATS
Population: 64,088,222 (July 2015 est.)
Urban Population: 82.6% of total population (2015)
Comparative Size: twice the size of Pennsylvania; slightly smaller than Oregon
Gross Domestic Product (per capita): $39,500 (2014 est.)
Gross Domestic Product (by sector): agriculture 0.6%, industry 20.6%, services 78.8% (2014 est.)
Government: constitutional monarchy and Commonwealth realm
Languages: English

SOCIAL PROGRESS SNAPSHOT
Social Progress Index: 84.68 (+23.68 above 61 world average)
Basic Human Needs: 92.22 (+23.89 above 68.33 world average)
Foundations of Well-being: 79.04 (+12.59 above 66.45 world average)
Opportunity: 82.78 (+34.55 above 48.23 world average)

The UK has historically played a leading role in developing parliamentary democracy. At its zenith in the 1800s, the British Empire stretched over one-fourth the world, but many British territories and colonies rebelled or were allowed to leave the Commonwealth. The UK's strength diminished after two world wars and the Irish Republic's withdrawal from the union. The empire was gradually dismantled, but the UK rebuilt itself into a modern and prosperous nation. A referendum scheduled for June 2016 was to decide if the UK would leave the European Union.

Conclusion

Europe as a whole has a strong economic foundation and provides a positive quality of life for most of its citizens. Still, recent events have stressed the economy and resources and challenged the spirit and character of the people who live there. Greece has been going through a period of great economic crisis, having taken on excessive debt with a great difficulty to pay back its creditors. Greece's troubles began a banking collapse in 2008 that sent the stock markets spiraling downward. When Greece announced that it had been understating its deficit for years in 2009, financial markets shut the country out from any borrowing. In 2010 the country was teetering on bankruptcy. Since that time, the European Union has been working with Greece to boost its financial health and stabilize the economy. Greece has been making steps toward repaying its loans, but the crisis has tested relations with the European Union.

In addition to turmoil in Greece, Europe has been coping with the biggest refugee crisis since World War II. Europe upholds asylum as a fundamental right. Asylum is granted to people fleeing persecution or serious harm in their own country and therefore in need of international protection. The new immigrants are fleeing countries in Africa and the Middle East that have been destroyed by war, dictatorial oppression, or religious extremism, such as Syria, Iraq, and Eritrea. More than a million migrants and refugees have crossed into Europe because of recent political unrest in the Middle East, and the flow of people out of this region is expected to continue as long as instability persists. Deciding how to deal with such a great influx of people has been a burden for European countries, but people are taking action to help bring in as many refugees as possible. Acts of terrorism, however, especially in France, have led to heightened tensions in Europe and increased opposition to refugees.

World Bank President Jim Yong Kim and German Chancellor Angela Merkel attend the UN Sustainable Development Summit in New York in September 2015. Kim, a medical doctor with a background in development, and Merkel strongly support the UN Sustainable Development Goals of eliminating extreme poverty worldwide, one of the world's foremost programs in the beyond GDP movement.

The statistical office of the European Union, Eurostat, reported that nearly 80 percent of European residents rated their overall life satisfaction in 2013 at 6 or higher on a scale of 0 to 10. Overall, countries appear to be on strong economic footing. Some countries that have been hurting economically appear to be gaining ground. Spain, for example, is bouncing back after having been through five years of recession. By August 2015 unemployment was decreasing, and its economy was expected to grow by 3 percent throughout 2015, compared to growth below 2 percent in Germany and France. With its record for defending human rights and providing basic human needs and education, Europe seems to be on a positive track for the near future.

Series Glossary

Anemia: a condition in which the blood doesn't have enough healthy red blood cells, most often caused by not having enough iron

Aquifer: an underground layer of water-bearing permeable rock, from which groundwater can be extracted using a water well

Asylum: protection granted by a nation to someone who has left their native country as a political refugee

Basic human needs: the things people need to stay alive: clean water, sanitation, food, shelter, basic medical care, safety

Biodiversity: the variety of life that is absolutely essential to the health of different ecosystems

Carbon dioxide (CO_2): a greenhouse gas that contributes to global warming and climate change

Censorship: the practice of officially examining books, movies, and other media and art, and suppressing unacceptable parts

Child mortality rate: the number of children that die before their fifth birthday for every 1,000 babies born alive

Communicable diseases: medical conditions spread by airborne viruses or bacteria or through bodily fluids such as malaria, tuberculosis, and HIV/AIDS; also called **infectious diseases;** differ from **noncommunicable diseases**, medical conditions not caused by infection and requiring long-term treatment such as diabetes or heart disease

Contraception: any form of birth control used to prevent pregnancy

Corruption: the dishonest behavior by people in positions of power for their own benefit

Deforestation: the clearing of trees, transforming a forest into cleared land

Desalination: a process that removes minerals (including salt) from ocean water

Discrimination: the unjust or prejudicial treatment of different categories of people, especially on the grounds of race, age, or sex

Ecosystem: a biological community of interacting organisms and their physical environment

Ecosystem sustainability: when we care for resources like clean air, water, plants, and animals so that they will be available to future generations

Emissions: the production and discharge of something, especially gas or radiation

Ethnicities: social groups that have a common national or cultural tradition

Extremism: the holding of extreme political or religious views; fanaticism

Famine: a widespread scarcity of food that results in malnutrition and starvation on a large scale

Food desert: a neighborhood or community with no walking access to affordable, nutritious food

Food security: having enough to eat at all times

Greenhouse gas emissions: any of the atmospheric gases that contribute to the greenhouse effect by absorbing infrared radiation produced by solar warming of the earth's surface. They include carbon dioxide (CO_2), methane (CH_4), nitrous oxide (NO_2), and water vapor.

Gross domestic product (GDP): the total value of all products and services created in a country during a year

GDP per capita (per person): the gross domestic product divided by the number of people in the country. For example, if the GDP for a country is one hundred million dollars ($100,000,000) and the population is one million people (1,000,000), then the GDP per capita (value created per person) is $100.

Habitat: environment for a plant or animal, including climate, food, water, and shelter

Incarceration: the condition of being imprisoned

Income inequality: when the wealth of a country is spread very unevenly among the population

Indigenous people: culturally distinct groups with long-standing ties to the land in a specific area

Inflation: when the same amount money buys less from one day to the next. Just because things cost more does not mean that people have more money. Low-income people trapped in a high inflation economy can quickly find themselves unable to purchase even the basics like food.

Infrastructure: permanent features required for an economy to operate such as transportation routes and electric grids; also systems such as education and courts

Latrine: a communal outdoor toilet, such as a trench dug in the ground

Literate: able to read and write

Malnutrition: lack of proper nutrition, caused by not having enough to eat, not eating enough of the right things, or being unable to use the food that one does eat

Maternal mortality rate: the number of pregnant women who die for every 100,000 births.

Natural resources: industrial materials and assets provided by nature such as metal deposits, timber, and water

Nongovernmental organization (NGO): a nonprofit, voluntary citizens' group organized on a local, national, or international level. Examples include organizations that support human rights, advocate for political participation, and work for improved health care.

Parliament: a group of people who are responsible for making the laws in some kinds of government

Prejudice: an opinion that isn't based on facts or reason

Preventive care: health care that helps an individual avoid illness

Primary school: includes grades 1–6 (also known as elementary school); precedes **secondary** and **tertiary education**, schooling beyond the primary grades; secondary generally corresponds to high school, and tertiary generally means college-level

Privatization: the transfer of ownership, property, or business from the government to the private sector (the part of the national economy that is not under direct government control)

Sanitation: conditions relating to public health, especially the provision of clean drinking water and adequate sewage disposal

Stereotypes: are common beliefs about the nature of the members of a specific group that are based on limited experience or incorrect information

Subsistence agriculture: a system of farming that supplies the needs of the farm family without generating any surplus for sale

Surface water: the water found above ground in streams, lakes, and rivers

Tolerance: a fair, objective, and permissive attitude toward those whose opinions, beliefs, practices, racial or ethnic origins, and so on differ from one's own

Trafficking: dealing or trading in something illegal

Transparency: means that the government operates in a way that is visible to and understood by the public

Universal health care: a system in which every person in a country has access to doctors and hospitals

Urbanization: the process by which towns and cities are formed and become larger as more and more people begin living and working in central areas

Well-being: the feeling people have when they are healthy, comfortable, and happy

Whistleblower: someone who reveals private information about the illegal activities of a person or organization

Index

RESOURCES

Continue exploring the world of development through this assortment of online and print resources. Follow links, stay organized, and maintain a critical perspective. Also, seek out news sources from outside the country in which you live.

Websites

Social Progress Imperative: socialprogressimperative.org
United Nations—Human Development Indicators: hdr.undp.org/en/countries and Sustainable Development Goals: un.org/
    sustainabledevelopment/sustainable-development-goals
World Bank—World Development Indicators: data.worldbank.org/data-catalog/world-development-indicators
World Health Organization—country statistics: who.int/gho/countries/en
U.S. State Department—human rights tracking site: humanrights.gov/dyn/countries.html
Oxfam International: oxfam.org/en
Amnesty International: amnesty.org/en
Human Rights Watch: hrw.org
Reporters without Borders: en.rsf.org
CIA—The World Factbook: cia.gov/library/publications/the-world-factbook

Books

Literary and classics

The Good Earth, Pearl S. Buck
Grapes of Wrath, John Steinbeck
The Jungle, Upton Sinclair

Nonfiction—historical/classic

Angela's Ashes, Frank McCourt
Lakota Woman, Mary Crow Dog with Richard Erdoes
Orientalism, Edward Said
Silent Spring, Rachel Carson
The Souls of Black Folk, W.E.B. Du Bois

Nonfiction: development and policy—presenting a range of views

Behind the Beautiful Forevers: Life, Death, and Hope in a Mumbai Undercity, Katherine Boo
The Bottom Billion: Why the Poorest Countries Are Failing and What Can Be Done About It, Paul Collier
The End of Poverty, Jeffrey D. Sachs
For the Common Good: Redirecting the Economy toward Community, the Environment, and a Sustainable Future,
    Herman E. Daly
I Am Malala: The Girl Who Stood Up for Education and Was Shot by the Taliban, Malala Yousafzai and Christina Lamb
The Life You Can Save: Acting Now to End World Poverty, Peter Singer
Mismeasuring Our Lives: Why GDP Doesn't Add Up, Joseph E. Stiglitz, Amartya Sen, and Jean-Paul Fitoussi
Rachel and Her Children: Homeless Families in America, Jonathan Kozol
The White Man's Burden: Why the West's Efforts to Aid the Rest Have Done So Much Ill and So Little Good, William Easterly

Foreword writer Michael Green is an economist, author, and cofounder of the Social Progressive Imperative. A UK native and graduate of Oxford University, Green has worked in aid and development for the British government and taught economics at Warsaw University.

Author Don Rauf has written more than 30 nonfiction books, mostly for children and young adults, including *Killer Lipstick and Other Spy Gadgets*, *The Rise and Fall of the Ottoman Empire*, and *Simple Rules for Card Games*. He lives in Seattle with his wife, Monique, and son, Leo.